Hattie's New House

Look out for other
LITTLE DOLPHIN titles:

Party Time, Poppy!
Milo's Big Mistake
Oscar's Best Friends
Fergal's Flippers
Sammy's Secret

And if you've enjoyed reading about
Little Dolphin and his adventures,
why not try reading the Little Animal Ark
books, also by Lucy Daniels?

Hattie's New House

Illustrated by DAVID MELLING

LUCY DANIELS

*Hodder
Children's
Books*

A division of Hodder Headline Limited

To Sarah Bertram

Special thanks to Jan Burchett and Sara Vogler

Text copyright © 2004 Working Partners Limited
Created by Working Partners Limited, London, W6 0QT
Illustrations copyright © 2004 David Melling

First published in Great Britain in 2004
by Hodder Children's Books

A Catalogue record for this book is available from the
British Library

ISBN 0 340 87346 9

Printed and bound in Great Britain by
Clays Ltd, St Ives plc

The paper and board used in this paperback by Hodder Children's
Books are natural recyclable products made from wood grown in
sustainable forests. The manufacturing processes conform to the
environmental regulations of the country of origin.

Hodder Children's Books
A division of Hodder Headline Limited
338 Euston Road, London NW1 3BH

CHAPTER ONE

Little Dolphin poked his nose out
of the water. It was a lovely
morning in Urchin Bay. The sun
was shining and the sea was
blue. It was a perfect day for
jumping.

Little Dolphin could see his
best friend, Milo, in the middle of
the bay. Milo was leaping out of
the water. He curved in the air

and then plunged back down through the waves. He made jumping look so easy!

Little Dolphin longed to be able to jump. He'd flipped his flippers and flapped his tail. He'd waggled his whole body until he thought his head would fall off! But he still couldn't do a jump. Not even a tiny one.

"Come on, Little Dolphin!" called Milo. He swooshed past backwards, balancing on his tail. "Remember – nose up, tail flip, wiggle! See that clump of seaweed at the end of the reef? Jump over that!"

"I'll try," Little Dolphin said. It was only a small clump of seaweed after all. He could easily jump over that! He gave Milo a determined smile and set off, swimming along the coral reef. A family of clown fish darted away to hide in the pink and orange fingers of coral as he skimmed past.

Little Dolphin could see the
seaweed straight ahead. It
looked a lot bigger now. Could
he really jump over that? He
could feel his heart pounding.
Little Dolphin put his nose up,
flapped his tail and wiggled.
Oh no! He was too close to
the seaweed. He shut his eyes

quickly, tried to
swerve and
plunged straight
into the waving
green leaves!
Milo pushed
the sticky weed
off his friend's

flippers with his nose.

"Bad luck, Little Dolphin," he said.

Little Dolphin sighed. "All the other dolphins I know can jump. Why can't I?"

"You will," said Milo. He gave Little Dolphin a friendly nudge with his tail. "Try flapping your fins harder."

"I'm flapping as hard as I can," Little Dolphin said.

"Could you wiggle a bit more?" asked Milo.

"If I wiggle any more I'll burst!" Little Dolphin wailed. "I know what I'm supposed to do, it's just that I get into a tizzy when I try."

Milo thought hard. "When I learned to jump, my brother Bertie gave me some very good advice," he said. "In fact, he told me never to forget it."

"Great! What was it?" Little Dolphin asked eagerly.

Milo thought again. Then he shook his head. "I've forgotten," he said.

Little Dolphin rolled his eyes. Milo was such a scatterbrain! "Well, my dad says I should just keep practising," he said.

Milo nodded. "Your dad

should know. He's been Urchin Bay's Jumping Champion three years running! His triple flips last Sports Day were the best!"

Milo rolled over and over in the water, scattering some passing angelfish. Suddenly he snorted with laughter. "That was a great day! Do you remember Poppy in the Junior Spinner Dolphin Race?"

"Oh yes," Little Dolphin said. "She spun so fast she got all dizzy and ended up with her nose stuck in a clam shell! It was so funny."

"The clam didn't think so!" whistled Milo.

Little Dolphin grinned. Milo always cheered him up. As he looked out across Urchin Bay he saw some more dolphins jumping and playing in the warm sun. "I'll have one more go," he decided. This time he was going to get everything right.

"Watch me, Milo!" Little Dolphin called, as he sped up

towards the surface of the water. He lifted his head ready to soar into the air – and then Little Dolphin forgot everything he'd been told. What should he do with his nose? And should he flap before he wiggled?

In a panic he flapped wildly, wiggled his nose, lifted his tail – and plunged straight to the bottom of Urchin Bay.

CHAPTER TWO

Ouch! Little Dolphin's nose hit
something hard and knobbly on
the sandy sea-bed. He darted
back, sending the sand swirling.

"Watch out!" said a grumpy
voice.

Where was the voice coming
from? Little Dolphin couldn't see
anything through the churning
sand.

"I'm uncomfortable enough without dolphins landing on me!" said the voice crossly.

Little Dolphin looked at the sea-bed. The sand was settling now but all he could see was a shabby brown shell amongst the pebbles. "Who's there?" he asked timidly.

"It's me, silly!" The shell gave a shudder. Then a snapping claw appeared, followed by a pair of beady eyes and two twitching whiskers. Hattie the hermit crab was peering out at him.

"Hattie!" Little Dolphin whistled in relief. "I didn't recognize you.

You're living in a new shell! I'm sorry I landed on you. You see, I'm learning to jump. And I keep getting it wrong."

"Well, I've got a much worse problem," said Hattie impatiently. "This morning I decided that my lovely white shell had grown too tight. I think I've been

eating too many sea slugs—"

Suddenly there was a yell and a scraping noise behind them. They turned to see Milo skidding along on his belly. He crashed straight into them. Little Dolphin and Hattie were sent rolling over and over, along the sea-bed.

"Did you like my skid stop, Little Dolphin?" Milo clicked happily. Then he spotted Hattie shaking her claws at him. "Oh, hello, Hattie. What are you doing in that ugly old shell?"

"That's what I'm trying to tell Little Dolphin," grumbled Hattie. She struggled out of her shell and stretched her stiff legs with a groan. Then she went on with her  story. "As I was saying, my white shell had grown too tight, so I was looking for a new home. That shifty shark, Vinnie, told me he had just the shell for me. It only cost two limpets and a barnacle. So I paid up, and he took my lovely white shell away. But he's tricked me! This brown shell is even smaller."

"And it's so scruffy, it looks like it's been in a fight with a swordfish!" whistled Milo.

Little Dolphin felt sorry for Hattie. He was glad dolphins didn't grow out of their caves and have to find new homes. "Let's play a game of hide and seek," he chirped.

"That will cheer you up."

"How can I play hide and seek when I've got to carry this heavy old shell about?" moaned Hattie. "I miss my shiny white one."

"Follow the leader, then?" squeaked Milo. "I'll go first." He began to twist in and out of the rocks on the sea-bed.

"I'm too slow in this horrible shell," complained Hattie. "Now if I had my white one…"

"Let's play noughts and crosses," Little Dolphin said quickly. "You don't have to move much for that." He drew a grid

in the sand with his nose.

"I don't want to play anything. I'm too uncomfortable!" Hattie snapped.

Little Dolphin felt a bit impatient with Hattie. "OK, Hattie," he said. "If you don't want to play, Milo and I shall do some jumping practice instead."

"I knew there was something we were meant to be doing!" whistled Milo.

Hattie struggled back into her tight brown shell. "Go on then," she muttered. "See if I care!" And she crawled awkwardly away.

CHAPTER THREE

Little Dolphin swam up to the
surface. "Nose up, tail flip,
wiggle!" he said to himself.
"Nose up, tail flip, wiggle ... or
is it nose flip, tail wiggle?" He
turned to ask Milo.

Milo was playing in the
waves, batting a red beach
ball between his flippers. He
had forgotten about jumping.

"Look what I've found, Little Dolphin," he called. "It must have washed out to sea. Let's have a game!"

But Little Dolphin still wanted to jump. He decided to go home and ask his mum for another lesson. He said goodbye to Milo, who was balancing the ball on his nose in front of a group of admiring seal pups.

Little Dolphin set off towards his cosy cave in the rocks on the other side of the reef. He swam along, feeling the sun on his back and sending spray up through his blowhole.

Soon he was swimming over the hole in the reef where Cornelius the conger eel lived. Cornelius didn't like to be disturbed. Was that a big grey nose coming slowly out of the hole? With a flick of his tail, Little Dolphin swam quickly away.

He stopped and looked back to make sure Cornelius wasn't following him. Suddenly,

he felt something pinch his tail!
Little Dolphin was really scared.
"Ouch!" he cried. Then he felt
another pinch – and this time it
was harder!

Little Dolphin lifted his nose,
gave his tail a sharp flick – and
shot clean out of the water up,
up, up into the bright sunlight!

CHAPTER FOUR

Little Dolphin couldn't believe it. He was jumping! It was a great feeling, soaring up towards the blue sky.

His landing wasn't so good though. He hit the water with a huge smack!

But Little Dolphin didn't care. He'd jumped! He had to tell Milo!

Then he remembered his sore tail. Had Cornelius nipped it? Was he still lurking nearby? Little Dolphin looked back anxiously towards the reef.

There on the coral stood Hattie the hermit crab. She was waving her claws crossly at him.

"Did *you* pinch my tail, Hattie?" Little Dolphin asked, in surprise.

"Yes, I did," snapped Hattie.

"But why?" Little Dolphin asked.

"Because I'm very uncomfortable in this *horrible* new shell," Hattie said. "And you don't care!"

"Yes I do, Hattie!" Little Dolphin squeaked. "And thank you for pinching my tail. It was very clever of you!"

Hattie's eyes stood out on their stalks. "What are you talking about?" she spluttered.

"When you pinched me," Little Dolphin said, "it surprised me so much that I jumped right out of the water. So now I know I really *can* jump. Look, I'll show you!"

Little Dolphin put his nose up, flapped his tail and jumped. He got halfway out of the water and fell back in with a splosh! "Now I'll show you a double twist just like my dad does." Flippers flapping wildly, Little Dolphin launched himself in the air, gave a twitch, and flopped back down in a storm of bubbles.

"And for my last trick," he called, "I'll—"

"Stop!" clattered Hattie. "You're making me dizzy!"

Little Dolphin looked at poor Hattie. She must be very unhappy in her cramped brown shell. No wonder she couldn't enjoy his jumping display. "I wish I could help you," he said. "After all, you helped me."

Milo was still playing about with the red beachball across the bay. "Shall we go and play with Milo?" he asked. "That might cheer you up."

"I can't!" wailed Hattie. "It'll take me all day to get there in this shell."

Little Dolphin thought it was a pity that Hattie couldn't do without her shell. But he knew that hermit crabs had to take their homes with them wherever they went.

Then he had a brilliant idea. "How about a ride?" he whistled. "Hang on to my fin and we'll be there before you can say lolloping lobsters!"

"I'll fall off!" clacked Hattie in alarm. "This shell isn't built for speed."

"I won't go fast," Little
Dolphin promised.

Hattie looked doubtful. "OK,"
she said at last. "But remember –
go slowly."

She climbed on to Little
Dolphin's back and gripped
his fin with both claws.
"I'm ready," she called.

Little Dolphin set
off, swimming
slowly
towards
Milo.

"Are you OK, Hattie?" he asked.
He could feel her pincers getting
tighter on his fin.

"Of course I am," said Hattie.
"Can't you go any more quickly?"

Little Dolphin grinned and
sped up.

"Yippee!" squealed his
passenger. "Faster, Little Dolphin!
Faster!"

They ploughed through the
water, Hattie clinging tightly and
yelling with delight.

In no time at all, they reached
Milo. "I'll surprise him," Little
Dolphin said. "Milo doesn't know
I can jump."

"Watch me, Milo!" he called.
And he launched himself out of
the water.

"Aargh!" clattered Hattie as
she lost her grip and went flying
high in the air.

CHAPTER FIVE

Oops! Little Dolphin had forgotten all about Hattie. She came down with a splash and sank to the bottom of the bay. Little Dolphin sped after her.

Hattie's shell was wedged in the sandy sea-bed. Little Dolphin could see her whiskers waving helplessly out of the top.

"Hattie!" he squeaked.

"Are you all right?"

For a moment there was no reply. Then Little Dolphin heard a hollow grunting sound from the shell. What could be wrong?

Slowly Hattie pulled herself out of her shell. Now Little Dolphin knew what the strange noise was. Hattie was laughing.

"That was great!" she gasped. She scrambled eagerly on to Little Dolphin's back again.

Little Dolphin swam up to the surface with Hattie. Milo whistled with delight when they told him the story of Little Dolphin's first jump.

"One day I'll be like my dad," Little Dolphin said. "The best jumper in Urchin Bay!"

"Never," said Milo with a cheeky grin. "Hattie will always jump higher than you!" And with a flick of his tail he was off. "Can't catch me!" he called as he charged through a family of surprised shrimps.

Little Dolphin sped after Milo, with Hattie on his back. Hattie held on tightly as they chased in and out of the seaweed. At last they sank down on some bouncy sponges.

"Thank you, Little Dolphin," said Hattie. "I've had a wonderful time. You really cheered me up." She clicked her claws and did a little dance in the sand. "In fact, I feel so much better I'm going to find that shifty shark Vinnie and tell him to give me back my limpets and barnacle. See you later." And off she went.

"I'm glad Hattie's cheered up," grinned Milo. "Race you to the wreck, Little Dolphin!"

"I've got a better idea," Little Dolphin declared.

"Let's play Hunt the Shell."

"Hunt the Shell?" said Milo, puzzled.

"We're going to find a new house for Hattie," Little Dolphin explained.

The two friends swam up and down, nosing in the sand.

"What about this?" called Milo. He nudged a rusty old can along the sea-bed.

"It's ever so modern and if she gets tired of walking she can close the lid and roll instead."

"Hattie won't like that!" Little Dolphin whistled. "Keep looking."

Milo grinned and poked about in some seaweed. Then he swam into a gap in the coral. "Help me with this, Little Dolphin!" he called as he wriggled out backwards.

Little Dolphin swam over. Milo was tugging at something long and thin.

"I've found a new kind of seaweed," Milo said.

Little Dolphin saw what Milo had in his mouth. "That's not seaweed!" he squeaked. "Quick, we have to hide!"

They darted behind the fronds of a large kelp bush.

Milo looked puzzled. "What's the matter?" he whispered.

"You were pulling Cornelius's tail!" Little Dolphin told him.

"Was I?" squeaked Milo in surprise.

"Yes, and now he's coming this way!" said Little Dolphin.

They sank down on to the sand and tried their best to look like seaweed-covered rocks

as the old conger eel slid past.
He had a grumpy frown on his
face and Little Dolphin was sure
he was searching for whoever
had pulled his tail.

Milo started to wriggle.

"Keep still," Little Dolphin
clicked. "He'll see us."

"But I've got an itchy nose!"
Milo clicked back.

At that moment, Cornelius
turned and swam towards them.
Little Dolphin and Milo froze.
They felt a swish of water as the
conger eel swam right over them,
muttering to himself.

After a while, they couldn't

hear him any more.

Little Dolphin risked a peek.
"He's gone," he sighed. "We'd
have been in trouble if he'd
found us."

But Milo wasn't listening. He
was rubbing his itchy nose all
over the sea-bed.

As he did so, Little Dolphin
could see something appearing
from under the sand.

CHAPTER SIX

Little Dolphin quickly flapped
away the rest of the sand. And
there in front of him was a shell.
A beautiful, pearly pink shell.
"You've found a house for
Hattie!" he whistled.

"Have I?" asked Milo in
surprise.

"Yes, you have," Little Dolphin
said. "We must give it to her!"

Balancing the shell carefully on his nose, Little Dolphin swam off to find Hattie, with Milo close behind.

The hermit crab hadn't got very far. "Wait, Hattie!" Little Dolphin called.

Hattie carried on inching her way across the sea-bed. "No time for playing now, Little Dolphin," she said.

"But we've got a present for you!" said Milo.

Hattie stopped and turned slowly round.

Little Dolphin put the shell down in front of her.

Hattie couldn't believe her eyes. "It's lovely!" she gasped. She scrambled out of her old brown one and scuttled into the lovely pink one. "And it's a perfect fit!"

"Now don't eat too many sea slugs!" grinned Milo.

Hattie pranced proudly up and down to show it off. "Thank you, Little Dolphin!" she said. "Thank you, Milo. I could win the Hermit Crab Marathon in this."

The two dolphins rubbed noses in delight.

"What are you going to do with the old one?" Little Dolphin asked.

Hattie looked thoughtful. "We'll give it back to Vinnie," she said at last. "I've thought of a great joke to play on that shifty shark."

Five minutes later, the three friends were watching secretly from behind a clump of sea

cucumbers as Vinnie the shark
danced in and out of his cave.
He was singing the Sharky
Sharks' latest hit as he decorated
his dinner with sea parsley.

"See my eyes flashing in the
dark!" he warbled happily. "Here
I am, I'm a sharky shark!"

"He's in a good mood!" Little Dolphin clicked. "Perhaps he'll give you back your limpets and barnacle if you ask him nicely, Hattie."

"I will," said Hattie, with a twinkle in her eye, "after we've played our joke. Ready, Milo?"

Milo was batting Hattie's old shell between his flippers in time to Vinnie's song. "Ready for what?" he asked.

"Our joke on Vinnie!" Little Dolphin hissed.

"Oh, yes!" grinned Milo. "I forgot!"

As soon as Vinnie went back inside his cave, Milo darted forward, hid the shell in Vinnie's dinner, and then dashed back to his hiding place. He was only just in time.

Vinnie glided out of his cave, his beady eyes glancing all around. Then he opened his mouth as wide as he could. The whole pile of food disappeared in one enormous bite.

Suddenly there was a loud *crunch*! Vinnie was so surprised he spat his dinner all over the sea-bed.

Now it was time for Little Dolphin's part of the plan.

He popped out from behind the cucumbers and swam around Vinnie, pretending to search for something. "Have you seen Hattie, Vinnie?" he asked. "She was having a nap – just here."

Vinnie's jaw dropped open. He looked at the remains of his dinner and spotted the bits of Hattie's old shell. In a panic he pushed them about with his nose. "Hattie!" he cried. "Speak to me, Hattie!"

He turned to Little Dolphin.

"Jumping jellyfish!" he gulped.
"I've eaten her. And she was one
of my best customers!"

Little Dolphin
couldn't stop
himself grinning.

"It's not
funny!" wailed
Vinnie.

"Yes it is!" said Hattie's
voice. She scuttled out of her
hiding place, followed by Milo.
Her whiskers twitched with
amusement.

"Hattie!" gasped Vinnie.
"You're alive!" Then he noticed
that the two dolphins were rolling

about with glee. "Hopping halibut!" he exclaimed. "You tricked me!"

"Just like you tricked *me* into buying that horrible shell this morning," snapped Hattie. "You knew it was too small for me."

"It's not my fault if you've grown since breakfast," blustered Vinnie. "What's all the fuss? You seem to have found a new one."

"No thanks to you!" said Hattie. "I want my limpets and barnacle back, please."

"I don't do refunds," said Vinnie. "But what about an exchange? I happen to have

a nice razor shell, just in. Only
one owner—"

"Don't be mean, Vinnie," Little
Dolphin clicked. "Give Hattie
what you owe her."

"She can't use her old shell,"
added Milo. "You've eaten it!"

"All right, all right!" said
Vinnie. "Don't get your flippers
in a twist." He swam into his
cave and came back with
two limpets and a barnacle.
He dropped them in front of
Hattie and gave her a toothy
smile. "While you're here,"
he said, "you might be interested
in a bargain." He produced a

small glass bottle. "Claw varnish," he explained. "Just your colour. And it's yours for only—"

"No, thank you," interrupted Hattie firmly. "I've had enough bargains for today."

"Fair enough," said Vinnie cheerfully. "Now if you ever want to sell that new shell, I'll give you a good price."

"I'm not parting with this one in a hurry!" said Hattie. "I want to go and show it to everyone. Can I have a lift please, Little Dolphin?"

"Hop aboard, Hattie!" Little Dolphin grinned.

"That was a great joke, Hattie!" said Milo, as the three friends swam along the reef.

"I'll never forget Vinnie's face when he thought he'd eaten me," Hattie clacked. "Thanks for helping, boys – and my new house is great."

"And thank you for helping me to jump, Hattie," Little Dolphin whistled.

"You may be able to jump!" said Milo with a grin, "but I bet you can't jump as high as me!"

"Bet I can!" Little Dolphin called. "Hold on tight, Hattie! We're off!"

And the three friends raced off to leap in and out of the waves.

LITTLE DOLPHIN: HATTIE'S NEW HOUSE

Now that you've finished this book, would you like another one to read, absolutely FREE?*

Your opinions matter! We've put together some simple questions to help us make our books for you better. Fill in this form (or a photocopy of it), send it back to us, and we'll post you another book, completely free, to thank you for your time!

Was this book ...
( ) Bought for you ( ) Bought by you ( ) Borrowed for you
( ) Borrowed by you

What made you choose it? (tick no more than two boxes)
( ) cover ( ) author ( ) recommendation ( ) the blurb
( ) the price ( ) don't know

Would you recommend it to anyone else?
( ) yes ( ) no

Did you think the cover picture gave you a good idea of what the story would be like?
( ) yes ( ) no

Did you think the cover blurb gave you a good idea of what the story would be like?
( ) yes ( ) no

Please tick up to three boxes to show the most important things that help you choose books:
( ) cover ( ) blurb ( ) author you've heard of
( ) recommendation by school/teacher/librarian/friend
(please delete the ones that don't apply) ( ) advert
( ) quotes on the front cover from well-known people

( ) special price offer ( ) being a prize-winning book
( ) being a best-seller

Which of the following kinds of story do you like most?
(tick up to three boxes)
( ) funny stories ( ) animal stories ( ) other worlds
( ) people like you ( ) people with special powers
( ) scary stories ( ) stories based on a TV series or film

How old are you?
( ) 5–6 ( ) 7–8 ( ) 9–11 ( ) 12–14 ( ) 15+

Name
Address

Please get a parent or guardian to sign this form for you if you are under 12 years old – otherwise we won't be able to send you your free book!

Signature of parent/guardian_____

Name in block capitals_____ Date_____

*Offer limited to one per person, per private household. All free books worth a minimum of £3.99. Please allow 28 days for delivery. We will only use your address to send you your free book and guarantee not to send you any further marketing or adverts, or pass your address on to any other company.

Please send this form to:
Reader Opinions, Hodder Children's Books, 338 Euston Road, London NW1 3BH.
Or e-mail us at: readeropinions@hodder.co.uk if you are over 12 years old.